The Ship and The Jungle

A Children's Story

By:

Dr. Darius M. Walker

Copyright © 2018 Darius Walker
This book is a work of fiction. Any names, characters, places and incidents are either products of the author's imagination or are used fictitiously. Any resemblance to actual events, locales or person, living or dead, is entirely coincidental.

All rights reserved. No part of this book may be reproduced in any form, including electronically or audio without permission from
Darius Walker Books

ISBN PB: 9781734193404
ISBN HB: 9781734193428
ISBN eBook: 9781734193411
Library of Congress Catalog Number:

Edited By: Alicia Ingram
Copyediting By: Omar Tyree
Proofread By: Amy S. Walker
Typeset By: Write on Promotions
Illustrator: Brian Allen, FlyLandDesigns.com

TABLE OF CONTENTS

PREFACE V
TESTIMONIALS VII
CHAPTER 1: "THE PURCHASE" 2
CHAPTER 2: "THE ARRIVAL" 8
CHAPTER 3: "FLOWERS OF ADAZEMENT" 16
CHAPTER 4: "THE FIRST NIGHT" 20
CHAPTER 5: "THE FIRST LEG" 26
CHAPTER 6: "QUESTIONS" 34
CHAPTER 7: "THE WAITING GAME" 40
CHAPTER 8: "THE SECOND LEG" 44
CHAPTER 9: "PEEK-A-BOO FLOWERS" 50
CHAPTER 10: "THE DESTINATION" 54
CHAPTER 11: "NOW WHAT" 60
CHAPTER 12: "COURAGE" 64
CHAPTER 13: "HOPE AND VICTORY" 70
CHAPTER 14: "GOING HOME" 76
THE END... 78
DR. DARIUS M. WALKER... 80

PREFACE

Writing this book was a mission to "See it Through!" Although I am a professionally trained scientist, I have a life-long relationship and love for creativity. Whether it be through the art of poetry, rap, or story-telling, I've longed to transition one of my creative ideas into a tangible project. Finally, I've reached my goal and proudly present to you, The Ship and the Jungle.

    The Ship and the Jungle is a story that takes a family of four on an unimaginable, adventurous journey to a strange place. Throughout their journey, the family is met with all sorts of challenges that require them to band together, persevere, and display courageousness in order to return home. The main characters are based on my two biggest inspirations for writing this book, my son and daughter. In fact, I use their given names, Toussaint and Kherrington, for the lead roles.

Most nights my wife, Amy, and I take turns putting the kids to bed. Kherrington and Toussaint almost always want to hear a story as they nod-off for the night. Often, we'll select a book to read but sometimes daddy is too tired to read; nevertheless, a story is still wanted. So, I'll dim the lights and begin conjuring up a story from my imagination until they fall asleep. In an unrelated conversation with a professional coach/mentor, Dr. Kathryn Burkgren, she suggested that I audio record and dictate ideas or memoirs. This gave me the idea to record some of the bedtime stories I created for my children and out of one of these stories, The Ship and The Jungle was born.

The first night, I thought of a topic or theme that the kids liked and pirate ships and adventures came to mind. From there, I "freestyled" my story-telling, adding to the adventurous journey of Captain Toussaint and his crew. Each night while telling the story, I conducted an audio recording until the chapter was complete. The following evening I'd ask Kherrington and Toussaint if they remembered where we left off and/or I'd listen to the final minutes of my previous recording in order to build on the story from there. Ultimately, I reached a point where I felt the story was finished. This resulted in 14 recordings which are now the 14 chapters of The Ship and The Jungle!

I'd like to thank my editor, Ms. Alicia Ingram, advisor, Mr. Omar Tyree, and illustrator, Mr. Brian Allen of Flyland Designs for helping to bring my vision to life. My most sincere, love and gratitude to my beautiful wife, Dr. Amy S. Walker, for her hands-on contributions and moral support of this project.

I hope you find the book entertaining!

TESTIMONIALS

"Darius really made what was once a bedtime story told to his children, come to life! The Ship and the Jungle combines family, fun and fantasy – and the colorful illustrations takes us on a visual journey led by Captain Toussaint. This story highlights important lessons of team-work, determination, and fearlessness which translate from the field to the classroom and beyond!"

Jahri Evans
-NFL Super Bowl XLIV Champion (2010),
6x Pro-bowler and 4x 1st Team All Pro

"The Ship & The Jungle is an instant family classic that will be shared for generations to come! Dr. Walker takes readers on a family voyage sailing through the waves of commitment and perseverance in a tale we can all relate to!"

Shawn Rux
-Deputy Superintendent
-NYC Department of Education

"The imagination is what allows us to see what others can't see, dream what others can't dream, go where others can't go, and become special. That's why it's so important that we support artists with imagination that give our children an experience that makes the impossible, possible while strengthening their outlook on life. What they could do? Who they could become? With The Ship & The Jungle, Dr. Darius M. Walker has given us a vessel for our children to imagine a special journey, a family adventure, an innocent opportunity to use their creative minds that will help them to grow into successful movers and shakers of tomorrow."

Omar Tyree
-New York Times bestseller and NAACP Image Award-winning author

Chapter 1

"The Purchase"

Kherrington slowly wandered around the tables and booths at the Saturday flea market, admiring a variety of new and old items that were for sale. There were unique and one-of-a-kind items in every corner; furniture, clothing, toys, electronics, and other knickknacks. Kherrington's younger brother Toussaint, age seven and nicknamed "Touy" for short, paused at a table that was loaded with toys.

"Kherrington, come look at this cool race car!" he said excitedly.

At the same time, their mom and dad began to call them from up ahead.

"Kiddos, come on. Keep up! There's a lot going on here, and we don't want you getting lost on us," their father told them.

The family had just moved into the neighborhood a week earlier, and they decided to hit the outdoor flea market to pick up a few odds and ends for their new home.

Kherrington and Touy turned and walked quickly to catch up to their parents. Kherrington's hair beads jingled and jangled as she skipped, *clickety-clack, clickety-clack* up the flea market's grass and dirt pathway.

Once the children caught up to their parents, they slowed their pace.

"So, now that Mom and Dad decided to let us stay in the same room, what's the first thing you wanna put in there?" Touy asked his older sister, only by one year.

Kherrington shrugged and thought about it, "I don't know, maybe a –"

"Eh 'dere, li'tal ones!" squawked an older West Indian woman, interrupting them. She sat behind a small booth with gray-haired dreadlocks, wearing a colorful island skirt. "Baby gal, me love your 'air!" she complimented Kherrington.

Amused and confused by it, Kherrington looked at Touy and giggled at the woman's lively accent.

"Air?" they both asked on beat.

"Yes, your *'air* with dem bright colored clickety-clacky t'ings," the woman replied, pointing to Kherrington's plastic hair beads. "And where is your mudder and faudder? Don't tale me ya' both in 'ere alone."

Before they could answer her, their parents approached the woman's booth.

"Hi! How are you?" their mother asked with a friendly smile.

"Ah, 'dare 'dey are! Good mornin'! What a *beautiful* fam'lee you dun 'ave. May I in'trest ya' in some items for 'de home?"

The family of four began to look around at an assortment of unusual things the woman had to sale.

"Look at this, dear!" their mother exclaimed to their father as she walked forward. "She has two twin-sized beds. And they're antiques in perfect condition! The kids could use some new beds now. Don't you think?"

Their father looked and nodded. He said, "Sure! Their old beds could be replaced.'"

Kherrington and Touy loved the beds so much that they began to jump up and down in excitement.

"Oh my Gosh! You see those cool beds, Touy?" Kherrington

inside and loved it.

"This is amazing! Look at how much room we have," Kherrington exclaimed as she climbed on top of the front end.

"Well, shiver me timbers!" their Dad joked.

Their Mom brushed her shoulders off proudly and said, "I sure do know how to pick 'em." She enjoyed the new boat beds as well.

"Wow. My very own pirate ship," Touy marveled in amazement.

Suddenly, Toussaint looked down as his socks felt damp and noticed the bedroom was actually beginning to fill with water. "Quickly everyone get ready! The tide is rising!" he shouted.

"Yeah, the room is flooding fast. Everyone hold on to something," his father added in.

Kherrington and her mother followed the orders and held on tightly to the edge of the beds. The walls of the room began to disappear as the water rose, and before they all knew it, they were out in the middle of the ocean on a real pirate ship.

Excited and confused, their father sat down on the ship's deck and said, "What's going on? What's happened? Where are we?"

Before anyone could answer, dark grey storm clouds began to fill the clear blue evening sky.

Captain Toussaint then took command. "Okay, mates! Stand up! We must act quickly. There's no time for sitting down! There's a storm rolling in fast from our starboard side. Everyone, man your stations now!"

The crew knew instinctively what to do. They began battling the incoming winds, pelting rain, and the relentless, pounding waves of ocean water. The ship swayed violently from side to side, but the crew held their ground.

As quickly as the storm had arrived, it soon departed, giving way to a clear night sky with a full moon. And the exhausted crew fell asleep with the calm midnight waters.

Chapter 2

"The Arrival"

At dawn, hungry and active seagulls circled the ship and began to squawk. First Mate Kherrington was already awake and manning her post in the ship's crow's nest while the rest of the crew overslept.

"Land ho, land ho!" Kherrington shouted as she rang the ship's morning bell.

The rest of the crew awoke in a hurry, including Captain Toussaint, and they all looked overboard to see that the ship was approaching an island. So the Captain ordered everyone to prepare the anchors.

"All right, Mates, get ready to go ashore! Anchors down!" he shouted.

After anchoring the ship close to the island, they each gathered a satchel of supplies and rowed a small canoe ashore.

They were greeted there by white sands that covered a magnificent beach. Fifty feet behind the sands of the beach was a lush jungle of towering trees. The crew, full of curiosity and excitement, entered the jungle and began to wander the island.

First Mate Kherrington ventured toward the tall trees until

she came upon a large stone that was almost as big as she was. The stone was waist high and as smooth as glass with hues of dark purple, black and gold.

Kherrington walked closer to admire the stone and get a better look at it when she heard an unfamiliar voice calling her name from deep within the jungle. Curious about it, she walked toward the voice, deeper and deeper into the darkness of the trees.

Not finding anything, right as she thought of returning to get her crewmates behind her, the dense jungle gave way to the most wondrous field of wildflowers that Kherrington had ever seen. There were flowers of every color imaginable, growing in the most amazing patterns. Then she heard the voice again, calling out her name from the bed of flowers, as she wandered farther into the field.

Kherrington danced along the colorful bouquets, touching and smelling as many of the beautiful flowers as she could. After a few minutes of her happy energy, she began to feel dazed and sleepy. Before she knew it, she fell to her knees, gently stretched her body out on the ground, and went into a deep slumber.

In a blink of an eye, it seemed as if several hours had passed while Kherrington continued to rest in the bed of flowers. She felt like she was in some kind of trance, as her mind and body hovered between awake and sound asleep, as if she was paralyzed. Was she dreaming?

Kherrington wasn't sure what to make of it. Finally, in the distance she heard her crewmates calling for her. She wanted to yell back to them, "I'm here! I'm right here!" But for some reason, she couldn't.

Kherrington tried as much she could to raise her head and shake her beads to respond to them. In her mind, she was shaking her beads as loudly as possible, but she soon realized that her body was not responding to her wishes.

The flowers had indeed put her under a spell.

It was well over two hours since Kherrington had disappeared from her shipmates. The crew was scouring around the island calling out her name, and they were tired and hungry. Nevertheless,

Captain Toussaint remained determined to find her.

"I don't care if we have to cover every inch of this jungle! We're going to find Kherrington," he declared. "Let's stop for a moment to think and devise a plan."

The second and third mate gathered around Captain Toussaint as he picked up a stick and began drawing out a diagram in the sand. He used a coconut shell to serve as the ship. He then placed a palm leaf in front of the shell to represent the jungle.

"Okay, we docked our ship here and this is the start of the jungle," he said, pointing to the leaf on the diagram. "Who left first?" he continued.

The crew thought about it and they all agreed that Kherrington had been the first to leave the boat.

"So which way did she go?" Captain Toussaint asked.

"That way!" his mom asserted, pointing to her right.

"No, she went that way!" his dad refuted, pointing in the opposite direction.

Captain Toussaint pointed in between both of their arms. "I know where she went. She went that way," he told them as he aimed toward a midpoint.

Out of the corner of his eye, and in the direction that he was pointing, Captain Toussaint spotted a tiny red object lodged in a tree branch near the dark stone. It resembled one of the small beads that Kherrington had worn in her hair.

"Brilliant, great job. You're absolutely the best!" his dad said, praising the captain for his sharp eye.

They all raced toward the red hair bead to see if they could find Kherrington.

With a clear direction to search, Captain Toussaint instructed his dad to move twenty feet to his right and mom to move twenty feet to his left.

"At that distance, we should all be able to see and hear each other where no one else gets lost," the captain explained.

He then picked up three seashells from the sand and gave one to each mate and kept one for himself. They each blew on their shells, which all made a different sound.

"Now we can all blow on our shell every ten paces so we know where everyone is," Captain Toussaint instructed.

With the captain leading the way, the crew moved deeper and deeper into the jungle, cutting away branches with the machetes that they found in their satchels. Eventually, the captain was able to see a field of flowers up ahead. But as he took a few more steps toward the field, he began to get sleepy. He didn't realize that he was falling into the same daze as Kherrington.

Fortunately, he wasn't close enough to fall into a paralyzing sleep like his sister. Rather than continue walking forward, he stopped and walked backwards. As he moved farther away from the flowers, he was able to shake off the daze. He then heard his second and third mates blowing their seashells. He blew his seashell whistle to let them know his location.

"Stay where you are," he warned his crew as he continued to walk backwards from the sleep-inducing flower bed. "I don't know exactly what happened, but I just saw this beautiful field of flowers and started getting really sleepy as I got closer."

He said, "I have a hunch that Kherrington is somewhere in that field of flowers. But we can't go closer or we'll fall into a trance."

The Captain ordered dad to run to the ship and retrieve his spyglass.

"Do you have any extra scarves?" the captain asked his mom and pointed to the scarf tied around her head.

"Yes, you know I do," his mother replied and dug into her satchel.

"Well, let's try to breathe through the scarves without getting sleepy," the Captain said. He grabbed the scarf from his mate and placed it over his face.

His dad returned quickly with the spyglass. The captain thanked him and peered through the device. He gasped in amazement as he got a closer look at the expansive flower garden.

Captain Toussaint continued to scan the field until he spotted something that was the same beautiful brown color of his sister

Kherrington's richly hued skin.

"I think I see her, but I can't be sure," he told his mates. He zoomed in and saw the sun reflecting off one of Kherrington's colorful hair beads. That convinced him that she was among the blue, green, purple and pink flowers. All they had to do was figure out how to get her out of the field without falling into a trance themselves.

Chapter 3

"Flowers of Adazement"

As the crew devised a plan to get Kherrington out of the sleepy, deepy, dopey flowers, Captain Toussaint looked all around the jungle to study his surroundings. He looked high and low before spotting a monkey sitting up in the trees watching them intently. As Captain Toussaint looked up, the monkey began making several gestures.

The captain took a closer look at the monkey through his spyglass. The monkey looked as if he was dancing. Confused, the captain passed the spyglass to his dad to have a look of his own.

"Can you tell me what that monkey is doing? Is he trying to tell us something?" he asked.

His dad was equally confused. "He just keeps spinning around in circles."

He passed the looking glass over to his wife.

The captain's mother looked into the spyglass and said, "It looks like he's pointing at his nose and covering it."

"The monkey is definitely trying to tell us something. So why don't we walk closer to him?" she whispered, not wanting to startle the animal.

As they moved slowly toward the monkey, it started swinging and jumping through the trees to meet them. A few feet away from each other, the crew and the monkey stopped and stared at each other nervously.

Captain Toussaint remembered the piece of beef jerky in his supply bag. He took the snack out and threw it toward the monkey as a show of friendship. The monkey picked up the snack, smelled it, and threw it back at the Captain.

"Monkeys don't eat meat. They eat fruit," his mom informed the Captain.

She then tossed an apple toward the monkey from her satchel. The monkey picked it up, took a big bite and grinned. Holding the apple in one hand, the monkey waved for them to follow him with the other. The crew followed him until they reached a big tree. The monkey stopped and started doing his strange dance again. He flailed around in circles while holding his nose. The crew still couldn't figure out what he was trying to tell them.

Failing at the first method, the monkey picked up a few of the large leaves from a nearby tree and began to wrap himself up in the leaves while making sure his nose was completely covered.

The monkey then rolled himself downhill into the bed of flowers past Kherrington. As he rolled through the flowers, the buds released a magical dust. Kherrington stirred briefly, opened her eyes, and then fell back to sleep.

At that moment, the crew figured out what the monkey was trying to tell them.

"I think we need to roll in a straight line over the flowers," the Captain suggested. "And when we get close enough, we all need to start yelling so we can wake our First Mate, Kherrington, from her sleep."

They quickly wrapped themselves in the leaves and rolled down the hill, following the monkey's example. As they rolled past Kherrington, who was still asleep, they shouted at her in unison, "Kherrington, wake up! Wake up!"

The magical flower dust flew everywhere.

Waiting at the bottom of the hill and past the field of flowers, the monkey began to make loud noises. *"Ooooh, ooooh, ooooh, aaaah, aaaah, aaaah!"*

As the monkey continued to hoot, Kherrington's eyes fluttered open again. Then she slowly sat up in a daze.

As the crew came to a stop beyond the flower bed, Captain Toussaint yelled, "Kherrington! Get up and run over here quickly!"

Still dazed but awake, Kherrington slowly crawled toward her shipmates. But just as she got close to them, she paused and laid back down again and quickly fell asleep.

Captain Toussaint unwrapped himself from the leaves. Trying another route, he covered his nose with his mother's scarf and inched back toward the flower bed to grab his sister. But as he got close enough to grab her, he began to fall asleep as well.

His dad then covered his nose and went back in to get both the Captain and Kherrington, until all of them were safely out of the flower bed.

"What happened? Where was I?" Kherrington asked through a yawn.

"We'll tell you all about it later. Come on, let's leave this place," Captain Toussaint said. He was already headed in the direction of the ship.

"Yeah, let's go," the monkey said, signaling for them to follow him in the opposite direction.

The crew stared at each other and then at the monkey. They were all amazed that he could speak.

"Let's go!" the monkey repeated with more urgency.

"But our ship is that way!" their dad protested.

Pointing to the setting sun, the monkey explained, "It's almost night time. If you thought those flowers were dangerous now, wait until the sun goes down. You'll never make it back to your ship in time."

"Okay. You've got us this far and saved my sister, so we'll follow your lead," the Captain stated.

The crew trailed after the monkey and went deeper into the jungle until they reached a towering cluster of trees.

"Welcome to my place!" the monkey said as he scurried up the wide tree trunk with ease. The crew began to climb the tree at a much slower pace behind him. At the top of the tree canopy was a makeshift tree house stocked with piles of fruit and nuts.

"Get comfy. You can stay here for the night, and I'll tell you all you need to know about the island," the monkey told them.

"All we need to know is how to get back to our ship and get out of here," their mother stated. She sounded irritated.

"Well," explained the monkey, "if you're here, you're here for a purpose and you can't leave until you've fulfilled your purpose."

None of them liked the sound of that, but it was nothing they could do but wait until the morning.

As the sun began to set, the crew watched in awe as the colors on the horizon changed from a brilliant yellow to a glowing orange. Then the clouds turned to a turquoise green before changing to purple.

"We've been so busy rolling through flowers, that I haven't properly introduced myself," the monkey said. "My name is Bingo Bananas, but my friends just call me Bingo."

"I'm Captain Toussaint. My friends call me Touy. This is First Mate Kherrington, Mate Mom, and Mate Dad," Captain Toussaint introduced them, pointing to each member of his crew and family.

"Nice to meet you all," Bingo said. "And help yourselves to some food. Hopefully, what I share with you will get you off of this island. But first you must discover and complete your mission."

Chapter 4

"The First Night"

Nighttime settled in as Bingo began his story. Plants began to glow with fluorescent colors as strange noises floated through the air. The wind blew through the trees, carrying faint whispers that called each of the crew member's names.

"Swish! Captain Toussaint."

"Did someone just say my name?" the Captain asked. The monkey chuckled. *"Ooh, ooh, ooh, eee, eee!"* he laughed.

"Swish! Kherrington, don't you want to come play in the beautiful, peaceful flowers again?"

"The flowers are calling me again!" Kherrington said to her mates.

"Mate Dad, there is so much to explore. Things beyond your wildest dreams," swished the whispering winds.

"Mate Mom, so many jewels to be found! More beautiful than your eyes have ever seen."

They all looked around startled and asked each other if they had each heard the words of the whispering winds.

The monkey grinned and let out a small laugh as he shook his head. "The whispering winds spoke to each of you separately and told you only what you wanted to hear."

"But I heard them all!" Bingo declared proudly.

"Why can you hear all the winds and we can't?" Kherrington asked.

"I drank the special water from the sacred spring that only runs at dusk, just moments before nightfall. The water is a fluorescent blue and trickles down the mountainside, touching all of the plants. It is the most magical and majestic water you'll ever see. But until you drink the magical water, none of you will be able to hear all that I hear and see all that I see on this island."

Bingo paused before continuing. "I wasn't always able to talk, you know," he said, while chewing on an orange from his stash of fruit. "Like you, I heard the special whispering winds which led me to the magical spring, and now I'm talking to you!"

The crew then agreed that they should go and get some of the water immediately.

"Now remember," Bingo cautioned, "this place is very different from where you come from, and this is only your first night. Besides, since you all have different desires, those winds would have you scattered all about, looking for your individual wants rather than working together.

"It'll have the Captain going North, Kherrington South, your dad East, and your mother West," the monkey told them. "And once you're separated at night, I can't guarantee you'll ever find each other again."

He concluded, "When you hear those whispering winds, it usually isn't something good."

Distracted by the night sky, the crew began to look outside the treehouse window at the waves of colorful flames that danced in the air. The flames twisted, turned and spiraled all about. Once again, the crew was in awe.

"Yes, that's pretty nice, but that's just one small thing compared to the amazing stuff you'll see after drinking from the fountains," Bingo predicted. "You'll be able to hear, taste and see things that you never thought possible! Heck, you may even be able to do things that you once thought were impossible!"

Captain Toussaint became eager to see for himself.

"Let's go. I'm ready to conquer this place now," he stated.

"Please, it's too dangerous for you right now," Bingo advised. "You need to get your rest, and then tomorrow we can plot our course to the fountain. But if we head there at night, you all might as well be deaf and blind, because you're not going to be able to see or hear everything until you drink the magical water."

He continued, "There are certain things that you won't see that will turn you into a rock, a plant, or even sand. And those whispering winds will take you away from your goal of getting off the island. There are plants that could snatch you, insects that may devour you, and other elements on this island that would put you to sleep for ten years or more.

"Oh, and the animals—there are animals that talk, walk, fly, and do things that I don't even want to tell you," he added.

Bingo pulled out a map and showed the crew the location of the fountain in hopes of discouraging them from leaving in the middle of the night.

"You see that? You couldn't possibly travel that far at night."

But the Captain studied the map and was still eager to try.

"How long will it take for us to get there?" the Captain inquired.

Bingo said, "It's at least a two-day journey, but I have a friend halfway between here and the fountain, where we could rest at night. But don't be fooled, it's dangerous in the jungle during the daytime, too."

Realizing they would have to start their journey that next morning, the crew began to fall asleep, one by one. And as each of them dozed off, the whispering winds called out to them again.

"Captain Toussaint, come your ship awaits you."

"Kherrington, don't you want to play in the flowers? Remember how wonderful it felt to sleep."

"Mate Mom, the most brilliant, shiny and sparkling jewels are here, but only if you come down that tree now."

They each slept while fighting the temptations of the whispering winds, except dad.

"Come Mate Dad, and I will teach you things that you never imagined possible..."

Hearing his name called, their father began to sleepwalk and climbed down from the tree in search of the whispering winds. Halfway down, he awoke to a buzz in his ear.

Insects flew around and stung him, causing him to scream in pain and wake up, where he noticed Bingo staring down at him.

"Hey, what are you doing? Get up here now!" Bingo yelled at him.

But their father couldn't move as he cried out in agony.

Bingo threw him down a rope with a protective cage attached to it.

"Quickly, get inside the cage!" he yelled.

Their dad crawled inside the cage as Bingo pulled him back up to the tree house.

A fluorescent, greenish-yellow sap oozed from their father's arm, where the insects had bitten him. Bleeding heavily from his arm, he continued yelling in pain.

"Stay calm. You are going to be okay," Bingo reassured him.

"I can't believe they are coming after them so soon. They just arrived!" Bingo thought to himself about the elements of the island.

"What were those things?" their dad asked the monkey. "I heard this vibrating sound like *fla-da-da-don, fla-da-da-don*, and the next thing I knew, I felt this sharp, stinging pain."

"Those are razor insects that come out at night. They can destroy you as you can see," Bingo answered. "Lucky for you, I have a potion that can heal your wound. So you should be okay, but we'll have to make it to my friend's place as quickly as possible tomorrow. Because if we are just one minute late, after the sun sets, they will come out and get us all."

Chapter 5

"The First Leg"

As the sun started to rise, sunbeams danced on the crew's eyelids. They felt the warmth from the sun's rays with orange and yellowish colors swirling about in the dark.

Still groggy and only half awake, no one was quite ready to get up.

Finally, Bingo awoke and stretched, taking command.

"Wake up, quickly! We must go now!"

One by one the crew reluctantly got up from their floor pallets in the tree house—everyone except for dad. Still recovering from his insect wound, he remained asleep.

"Wow! I had the most amazing dream," Mate Mom said as she stretched and yawned. "I had so many jewels. I had a crown covered in diamonds, rubies and emeralds—even more beautiful than Queen Nefertiti's crown."

Bingo overheard her and clapped anxiously. "Shake off all your dreams and let's get going! We need to get your dad up and moving now. He is going to slow us down because of his wounds."

The crew was puzzled. They had slept soundly through the whole ordeal.

"Wounds? What happened to him?" Captain Toussaint asked.

"He followed the voices of the whispering winds and got introduced to the razor insects! Luckily, they only got one or two hits on him before I was able to pull him back into the treehouse. Any more would have been deadly!"

Understanding the urgency to start their journey, their mother suggested the smell of food as a way to stir her husband from his sleep.

Bingo grabbed a few eggs from his stash and gave them to their mom to prepare a quick breakfast meal. As soon as she began to cook, the smell of the food drifted through the air and their mate awoke.

"Is that breakfast I smell?" he asked, still grimacing in pain.

"Yes it is, dear" their mom replied with a smile.

"Great! Well, now that you're awake, let's move quickly," Bingo said hastily. "Remember, we have to make it over the mountaintop before nightfall. It's at least a half day trip and with your injuries. I'm not sure we'll make it in time."

They all ate their food quickly as instructed, then they filled their canteens with water and packed snacks for the journey. Bingo pulled out a map and showed them the route again.

"If for any reason someone is separated from the group, get back on the path immediately. If you can't find the path, look to the mountain. Once you see the red tree, head straight toward it."

By midmorning, the sun was well above the horizon when Bingo and the crew hurried down the tree. They then tied a rope around their dad and hoisted him down.

"Let's go! Let's go!" Bingo yelped. He flailed his arms, gesturing to the crew to speed up their movements.

Captain Toussaint grabbed his dad's arm and wrapped it around his shoulder to ease the pain. His dad was already struggling to keep up.

"Don't worry," he said reassuringly to his dad. "We're going to make it there and make it on time."

The crew couldn't help but admire the beauty of the jungle

as they hurried along. The shapes, colors and scents of the plants were like nothing they had ever seen or smelled before.

Kherrington breathed the air in deeply. "Mmmmm, I smell vanilla and chocolate! What is it? Where is it coming from? Let's go find it!"

Their mother smelled it too. "Yes, let's go find that deliciousness!"

"No, no, no… it's another *trick!*" Bingo shouted shaking his head. "Remember what happened when you followed those flowers, Kherrington? We must stay on the path to the red tree."

Saddened that they were unable to explore the chocolate and vanilla aromas that floated in the air, the crew started to slow down and complain.

Bingo reminded the crew very sternly of their mission and the dangers that they faced if they didn't move quickly.

Still unhappy with it, everyone straightened out their faces and began picking up the pace. They walked and walked for hours until they spotted the red tree in the distance. But as they got closer, it seemed as if the tree was moving farther away.

The crew was getting tired and their dad began to move slower and slower behind them. Sensing their exhaustion, Bingo showed everyone a place to rest.

"This is a good spot with a clearing all around us. We can see anything coming our way."

The crew stopped for a break. Bingo gave their dad some more of his homemade medicine and told the crew to eat their snacks quickly.

"We can only rest here for twenty minutes," Bingo warned them all.

"Twenty minutes?!" they complained.

"We've been walking for *hours,*" their mother said.

Bingo ignored their whining.

As they ate, Bingo took the old bandages off their dad and replaced them with new ones. Their mom saw the wounds for the first time and became very concerned about them.

"I've never seen scars like those before," she stated. The raised wounds oozed with fluorescent green pus. She then reached out to touch his scar. Bingo swatted her hand away before she could make contact with it.

"Don't touch it! It has to heal," he scorned her. "If you touch the wound, it may get worse and it could even infect you. Come on, it's time to go."

As they began to pack up, the crew noticed that the captain was suddenly missing.

"Captain Toussaint! Where are you? What are you doing?" Kherrington yelled.

A few feet away from the clearing, Captain Toussaint surveyed the land through his looking glass to find the source of the vanilla and chocolate aroma. Bingo ran toward him quickly and smacked the telescope from his hand.

The Captain looked at Bingo as if he was crazy for nearly breaking his spyglass.

"Captain! Stay focused. You're the leader of this crew and if you can't focus, none of them will."

"But that smell is incredible!" the captain whined.

"Yes, I know, but you can't be pulled into that temptation. Look what happened to your dad after he followed the enticing voices of the whispering winds!"

Heeding Bingo's wisdom, Captain Toussaint refocused and returned to the clearing to rejoin the crew, and they began walking again.

As more hours passed and they all moved farther along their path, a feeling grew stronger and stronger that someone or something was following them. But every time they looked back, they didn't see anything.

Suddenly, they heard rustling coming from a nearby bush. The noise grew louder and louder as the bush began to shake furiously. Then a huge rhinoceros with graffiti-patterned skin emerged while running with unusual speed. It knocked bushes and trees out of its path while heading directly for the crew who stood frozen in terror. But when the rhinoceros ran right past them, the crew sighed with relief.

"It looked like something was chasing him," Kherrington commented, still shaking with fear.

"What do you think he's running from?" she asked Bingo.

"I don't know and I don't want to find out. Let's keep it moving!" he advised them all.

The crew continued on their way and moved faster, propelled by the fear of the unknown until they reached the bottom of the mountain that they still had to climb. By that time it was already after midday. It seemed impossible to make it over the mountain with only six hours of daylight left. Everyone was exhausted and their mother's feet were hurting.

Captain Toussaint looked weary, but he remained focused on the mission. "If we need to go, I'll rally the crew," he said confidently to Bingo.

Bingo nodded. "Let's keep it pushin'."

The crew groaned and began hiking up the steep mountain. They moved slowly and carefully along the rocky terrain. One false move and any of them could slip and tumble back down the hill. So they pushed past the rocky area and came upon a muddy patch. Trudging through the mud wore them out even more. Bingo then suggested that they sing a song to keep going.

At the top of his lungs, Bingo belted out, *"Whooooaaa, I'm a work-innng, I'm a jump-innnngggg, I'm a hop-piiinnngggg, I'm a roll-ii-ingg up this mountain-nn, up this mountain-nnn … I'm a workinnnng, I'm a jump-innnng, I'm pulling, pulling, pulling up this mountainnnnn, up this mountain!"*

Everyone started singing along with Bingo, as the song lifted their spirits and filled them with energy. They started moving faster and got closer to the top. And as they sped up their pace, the sun began to sink behind the horizon. The crew then arrived at the red tree. Finally!

"We made it!" their dad said, relieved by it.

"We made it to the tree, but we still need to get over the top of the mountain and down to the other side," Bingo announced. "Time is running out. The jungle is starting to change," he warned.

They could see the colors of the sky changing again to the various hues that they had witnessed the night before.

"If we can make it to the top, I have a quick way back down," Bingo said, scurrying to the front to lead the way. "Come on, we need to hurry! Double time!"

He started to sing again.

"I'm a work-innng, I'm a jump-innnngggg…"

They were almost at the top of the mountain when Captain Toussaint told Bingo, "I still feel like something is following us."

"You're right, something is following us," Bingo whispered. "You can't see it, but I can. So we have to keep moving.

"We are almost there."

A few minutes before nightfall, the crew started to hear all kinds of noises again.

"Fladdddon, Fladdddon."

The drowning sound began to get louder.

Their dad grew frantic. "They're here! They've found us! The razor insects are back!"

"Please, calm down," Bingo said. "Yes, they are getting close, but they aren't that close. Come on, this way."

Bingo led them to a path that was covered with snow and mud on the other side of the mountain.

"We'll slide down!" he informed the crew.

They slid down the mountainside, and at the very bottom was a cave.

Pointing ahead, Bingo asked them, "You see that cave. That's my friend's place. Run toward it as fast as you can!"

Bingo let out a loud *"Ut-ut-ut-ah-ah-ah,"* monkey noise.

The cave door began to roll open. As they got closer to it, they started to see the razor insects, animals and plants that were responsible for all the weird and loud noises that was swirling around the entrance. Captain Toussaint trailed a few steps behind to make sure his crew all made it into the cave safely. Each member of the crew, along with Bingo, slid into the cave one by one.

Just as the captain began sliding in, a razor insect buzzed by and nicked him on the back of his leg. With no time to stop, Captain Toussaint ignored the pain and slid into the cave while the stone boulder quickly closed the entrance behind him. As he glanced back, he could only see the shadow of a large claw.

Chapter 6

"Questions"

Bingo jumped around the cave, screaming with excitement.

"That was amazing! I can't believe we made it!"

"I think I got stung by a razor insect. My leg is burning," Captain Toussaint grunted.

Suddenly his mother screamed, "A beeearrrr!"

In all of their excitement, no one noticed the huge brown bear who stood on his hind legs in the cave's dimly lit corridor that led deeper into the cave.

"Gizmo!" Bingo shouted in delight as he ran to greet his friend. The crew breathed another sigh of relief.

"Giz, these are my friends; Captain Toussaint, First Mate Kherrington, their mom and their dad."

Bingo pointed to each nervous crew member standing behind him.

"Hello, and welcome to my home," the large bear said in a deep booming voice that matched his stature.

Gizmo noticed the captain still holding his leg in pain.

"Come, I have something that will fix you up," he said

and motioned for the captain to follow him farther into the cave. He then applied a soothing cream to his infected leg.

Pulling back the fur on his arm, Gizmo showed the captain his own razor insect scars. "They hit me up too."

Later in the evening, the noises of the night grew louder. The thing that had followed them to the cave was clawing at the door.

"Don't worry," Gizmo assured the crew. "We're safe and secure in here. Nothing is getting in and nothing is getting out."

Hoping to get their minds off the noises, Gizmo offered them some food.

"You all must be starving. Want something to eat?

Their dad responded quickly, "What is that? It smells so good. I'm so hungry I could eat a bea-. Uhhh, I mean… I could eat a big bowl of whatever you're cooking."

"It's grilled fish and my special stew," Gizmo said with pride while stirring his stew.

"I never smelled that spice before," their mom said as she walked closer to the stove and peered around Gizmo's massive right shoulder.

"I hope it tastes as good as it smells to ya'," Gizmo said.

Bingo walked up to the stove, stuck his finger in the pot, and placed it in his mouth with a slurp. "Yupperz! It's as good as it smells."

Gizmo served everyone a bowl of stew as they gathered around the table. They all began eating, slurping and telling each other how much they all enjoyed the food.

"This fish is the best ever!" their mother exclaimed.

Gizmo was flattered.

"I think you all are just hungry from the long journey. It looks like you made it here in record time," Gizmo told them all. "Usually the journey from Bingo's place is a full day-and-a half trip."

"Yes, we did!" Bingo said between slurps of stew.

The crew eyed Bingo, puzzled and angry.

"You told us it was a *half* day trip!" Captain Toussaint said.

Feeling remorseful, Bingo started to explain himself. "If I told you the actual trip time, you may not have come. I had to keep you guys encouraged, and it wouldn't have been safe at my place for much longer."

In order to help out his friend, Gizmo quickly changed the subject.

"Tell me, friends, how did you all end up on this island?"

"We're not quite sure," Captain Toussaint answered. "We were sailing to Hispaniola when there was a sudden storm and our compass went haywire. Next thing we knew, we were here."

"Can you tell us why we're here," their dad inquired. "Bingo told us that if we were brought here it must be for a purpose, and we can't leave until the purpose has been met."

"I can't understand how or why the island would lure us here. We're just sailors," said an irritated Kherrington.

"Well, you all must be more than sailors," Gizmo suggested.

"So, what's next? Where do we go from here?" their mom asked.

"Well, I think we'll just rest up here for a day or so. The razor insects and that thing that's hanging outside the cave will probably get tired of waiting and leave after a while," Bingo said. He stood next to Gizmo and helped him clear the dishes.

"Yeah, that *thing?* What is that?" Captain Toussaint asked.

"We'll tell you all about that later," Bingo answered. "Right now, you should all just rest up and allow the Captain and your dad to recover from their wounds. Then we can make our way to the magical fountains so you can see and hear all that this island has to offer. Doing so may also reveal your true purpose for being here."

The crew agreed and retired for the night. But Bingo and Gizmo stayed up until everyone fell asleep. Once all of the crew members were asleep, they went to another part of the cave to talk.

"Giz, I really don't know what's going on here," Bingo whispered to his friend. "I've never seen the razor insects focus in on something so fast and so strong. I've never seen The Sashquashawon or the razor insects this interested in any visitors."

"That was The Sashquashawon outside my door?" Gizmo

asked, frightened and alarmed. His voice rose slightly above a whisper when he said it.

Bingo nodded and continued whispering. "They must be here for what we've all been waiting on. They're the ones who are going to free us!"

Gizmo became giddy with excitement at the possibility.

He said, "To be free would be amazing!"

Bingo motioned for his friend to lower his voice and not wake up the crew.

He said, "I know Dr. Z has ordered the razor insects and The Sashquashawon to come after the crew. There's no one else it could be. Thankfully the magical fountains are more powerful than even Dr. Z.

"So, come on, let's rest up. Tomorrow we can take the secret tunnel exit from the cave," Gizmo suggested. "That way, it'll only be about a half day trip to the fountains, and we can make sure those razor insects and The Sashquashawon don't see us when we leave."

Chapter 7

"The Waiting Game"

*T*hroughout the night, everyone could hear the razor insects buzzing outside of Gizmo's cave, while the Sashquashawon roared and scratched at the door. But eventually, everyone fell asleep, including Gizmo and Bingo.

They slept, slept and slept some more, far longer than they expected.

Gizmo woke up first, but it was well after dawn and he realized they had all overslept. "Oh man, there's no way we'll be able to make it to the other side of the island today and still have enough daylight to reach the fountains." He said loud enough to wake everyone.

Bingo looked out of the cave's peephole to see if he spotted the razor insects or The Sashquashawon. He was feeling antsy and wanted some fresh air.

"I don't see anything. Let's go outside for a bit and stretch our legs."

"Are you crazy?" Gizmo snapped at him. "It's a *trap*. They're still out there alright, and the Sashquashawon can smell us from miles away."

While their dad's wounds healed nicely, Captain Toussaint was still injured. So they decided to eat, rest, and sleep some more before heading out to the fountains through the secret tunnel the next day.

Later in the day, the crew began to get restless. They were sick and tired of being inside. So their dad stood up and started marching toward the door declaring.

"I wanna go outside!"

Captain Toussaint wanted to venture outside as well, but he knew not to.

"That thing called The Sashquashawon is out there waiting," he said. "I just know it. I can *feel* his presence."

Everyone managed to settle back down. They sang songs and told stories and eventually fell asleep for the entire night.

Very early that next day, Bingo awoke first while it was still dark. He gathered one small item of clothing from everyone and placed it near the cave entrance. He wanted to trick The Sashquashawon into thinking that they were still inside the cave as they moved through the secret tunnel.

When he woke everyone up, he told them to gather food and supplies for their journey. And once everyone was ready, they followed Bingo to another room in the cave that was filled will all sorts of artifacts. Gizmo led them to a large painting of a distinguished gentleman on the very same island that they were trying to escape. From the looks of his clothing and posture, he clearly was a man of importance. He banged on the wall three times, pulled a doodad and wiggled his tail against a lamp on the cave wall. Then the painting started to move to the right of the wall, revealing the entrance to the tunnel.

They crawled into the narrow passageway one by one. Bingo lit a candle inside as Gizmo did the same. Gizmo then led the team from the front while Bingo followed from the rear.

After a few hours of crawling, a breeze swept through the

tunnel with a *swoosh* and blew out their candles.

"Drats!" Bingo cried. "There goes my light."

They kept moving forward in the pitch-black tunnel. Eventually their eyes started to adjust to the dark and they could see a little better. Out of nowhere, they began to see the most amazing display of colorful gems. There were pink, purple, green and blue jewels. The light from the jewels shimmered off of the crew's skin, lighting their path.

After several hours, they started to get tired. The pretty gems started to fade away, and everyone became discouraged except for Gizmo.

He said, "I think it's a good sign. I think we're nearing the end."

The crew grumbled a bit more but continued onward. They crawled until they saw a hint of sunlight.

Their dad yelled, "Hey, I see some light!" And his voice echoed inside the tunnel.

Bingo quickly covered his mouth. "Shhhh. We don't want anyone or anything to know that we're here."

They crawled faster and faster toward the light, which grew larger and brighter as they neared the end of the tunnel.

Chapter 8

"The Second Leg"

"*E*veryone stay here. I'm going to peep the scene," Gizmo told them once they reached the end of the tunnel. He approached the tunnel's opening cautiously. He then stuck his nose out and began to sniff his surroundings.

"Well, it smells clear. I can't smell The Sashquashawon."

He peeked his whole head out to look around. He then inched the rest of his massive body out of the tunnel.

Once he was out, Gizmo walked around outside and found that their escape was safe. But he still wanted to be cautious and quiet.

"Bingo," he whispered. "Come here. Look at this."

Bingo moved over to him slowly and looked around, just as cautiously. He was confused and surprised.

"Where's the jungle?"

From inside the cave, Captain Toussaint could see Gizmo and Bingo's confused faces. He left the cave to join them.

"What's going on? What happened? Where are we?" Captain Toussaint demanded.

"We're not sure," Gizmo replied. "Last time I came this way, the tunnel led to the jungle. Now we only see a desert."

"What about the fountains? Are they still here? You told us we needed to get to the fountains so we can fulfill our purpose and get out of here," Captain Toussaint said angrily. "The fountains have to be here. They must."

"If the fountains are still here, they're that way," Bingo said, pointing to the left.

"No, no," Gizmo refuted. "They're to the right."

"Left!" Bingo repeated with more certainty.

"Right!" insisted Gizmo.

The captain shook his head and looked down at his feet in despair. He was angry and wanted to shout, but instead he said nothing and listened to his new friends as they continued to argue.

"Do you remember when we went this way last time? We walked toward the berry tree," Gizmo said. "I'd always eat some of those berries. And oh, how I *love* those berries. In fact, I could go for some berries right now."

Bingo folded his arms. "Yeah, we'd go to the berry tree but it was over that way and then we'd go over the hill."

The captain's eyes glimmered with a ray of hope as he spotted a sand dune in the middle of where Gizmo and Bingo were pointing.

"Well, maybe that sand dune is your hill," the captain suggested. "I have a hunch that the sand dune is the hill and we need to make it there quickly."

"Aye, aye Captain!" Bingo and Gizmo said in unison as they upright saluted him.

By then, the rest of the crew had made it out of the tunnel and watched from a few feet away. They, too, were in shock to learn that the jungle was missing. They listened to Captain Toussaint as he calmly explained that Bingo and Gizmo believed the fountains were over the sand dune. So their best chance of getting back to their ship and headed back home was to stay the course and find the fountains.

The crew all agreed and prepared themselves to leave.

The captain instructed them to drink their water sparingly and cover their heads with the scarves to protect them from the heat of the sun. Gizmo then covered the secret entrance to the tunnel so no one could find it.

They began their trek toward the dune as the sun grew hotter and stronger. The crew became more tired and discouraged with each step. There was nothing to be seen for miles except for an occasional cactus.

Captain Toussaint decided to sing to lift everyone's spirits. *"Mar-rrr-chiiiingg, ma-rrrrr-chiiiing, ma-rrrrr-chiiiing throooough the des-eeeerrrt. Ma-rrrrr-chiiiing, ma-rrrrr-chiiiing off to find the fountains."*

The crew began to sing along reluctantly. Their voices rose as they picked up their pace from a slow drag to a purposeful march.

When their energy began to wane, Captain Toussaint shouted, *"Whooo-ooohh!!! Weee'reeee maaarrrching, maarcchingg, maarrchingg through the desert. Maaarrrching to the founnnn-tains, Go-nnnnna fiiii-nd our waaaay back hoooome."*

This song uplifted the crew for miles, but eventually they began to get tired again.

As they walked, Kherrington and her mother spotted a single, small red and white flower sticking out of the sand. Their mother kneeled down and gently rubbed her fingers across its petals in admiration. Then she gasped in surprise as the flower quickly snapped itself shut with the quickness of an umbrella and disappeared back into the sand.

Its disappearance made her feel sad. She was so sad that she began to sing a song about the flower. And as she began to sing, the flower returned from the sand. Delighted, their mother continued to sing as more flowers and plants rose out of the ground. Trees and brushes began to sprout too.

"Keep singing," their dad advised her.

As she continued singing, Gizmo and Bingo started to recognize their surroundings as the familiar jungle returned.

"We're going the right way," Gizmo said, nudging Bingo.

"There's the rock and tree!"

Everyone was amazed. Even after their mother stopped singing, the plants remained above ground. They began to feel confident that they were indeed on the island for a particular purpose. They were ready to continue, but as they looked into the distance, they saw something coming fast in their direction. It was something dark, huge and furry, running wildly toward them.

From a distance, it appeared to be The Sashquashawon.

The ground under them rumbled as the beast moved closer. All the plants, flowers and trees hid back underground. And the crew, with Bingo and Gizmo, gathered their things and took off running themselves.

Chapter 9

"Peek-a-boo Flowers"

*T*hey ran toward the sand dune as fast as possible to get as far away from the beast as they could. They ran until their bodies were exhausted and out of reach from the creature.

Feeling excited and encouraged that they were safely away from The Sashquashawon, their mother began to sing again. The plants, trees, and flowers returned, giving Bingo and Giz their familiar landmarks.

"Captain Toussaint, thanks for showing us the way. We're both sure the fountains are just over this hill!" Bingo chimed excitedly.

As they approached the peak of the hill, the crew turned around to see if anything was following them. At first they saw nothing. But then they saw something moving slowly toward them. It resembled The Sashquashawon. But it wasn't roaring. It moved slow and seemed off balance.

Bingo squinted his eyes and sighed with relief. "That's not The Sashquashawon. It's just a Wooly Tuley."

"A Wooly Tuley?" Kherrington asked.

Bingo smiled. "Yeah, a Wooly Tuley. They are really friendly and nice. They're kind of like elephants but are covered in fur. It won't do anything to harm us. In fact, it might even help us."

Bingo crawled toward the approaching Wooly Tuley and began talking.

"What's your name?"

The Wooly Tuley just sat there and blinked. Bingo shrugged his shoulders and continued talking.

"My friends and I are heading to the magical fountains. Would you mind giving us a ride?"

Finally, the Wooly Tuley replied with a booming voice, "I'm trying to make it to the fountains, too. So if you all know the way, sure I'll give you all a ride."

The crew stared up at the mammoth sized Wooly Tuley. How were they going to get up on its back? Before they could figure it out, Bingo grabbed onto the Wooley Tuley's fur and pulled himself up.

"Hey that hurts!" the Wooly Tuley yelped.

Bingo quickly apologized. The Wooly Tuley then kneeled down and stretched out his trunk to give the others assistance. They each hopped on his trunk and walked up toward his back.

"Just don't kick me in the eye as you climb up," the Wooly Tuley warned.

Once they were all on his back, he instructed them to hold on tight to his fur. The Wooly Tuley then started walking and headed in the wrong direction.

"No, no straight ahead," Captain Toussaint said.

The Wooly Tuley turned and followed the Captain's instructions.

As they rode along, Bingo asked the creature his name for a second time.

With sadness, the Wooly Tuley said, "Well, ya see, I don't know what my name is or if I have one. I can't remember. That's why I need to get to the fountains."

Bingo felt sad for his new friend. He said, "I understand. Well, these mates were lost at sea," and pointed to the crew behind him.

"They have to get to the fountains so they can make it back home."

Bingo then came up with an idea in the hopes that it would comfort the Wooly Tuley. "Hey, why don't we just call you Tuley?" he suggested.

"Yeah I like that," Captain Toussaint chimed in. "It sounds just like my nickname, Touy."

The Wooly Tuley thought for a minute before smiling. "Yeah, Tuley. I like that too," he said.

As they moved along on Tuley's back toward their destination, everyone began to hear the splash and roar of water. That's when they all got excited.

Kherrington exclaimed, "The fountains! Do you hear the water? It must be the fountains!"

That made Tuley move faster and faster until he got stuck in some quicksand. Tuley bellowed and moved about wildly but it only made him sink further.

The crew tried to calm Tuley down but it didn't work. So their mother began to sing again to calm his spirit. The trees came out of their hiding places and grew tall, allowing Bingo to leap onto their branches. From the treetops, he inspected the ground around the area.

"Looks like dry land over there!" he shouted.

The Captain advised Bingo to take a branch and poke the ground to find where the dry land began and the quicksand ended.

Tuley calmed down as the crew patted him on the back and assured him that they would all make it out of the quicksand.

Surveying the ground from Tuley's back, their dad saw some vines close to the tree where Bingo was standing.

"Bingo, do you see those vines? Throw them over here."

When the crew got a hold of the vines, they braided them into a rope and threw it to Bingo. Their dad instructed Bingo to wrap the braided vines around the trunk of the tree and return the other end to Tuley, creating a pulley. The crew tied one end around Tuley's back and front legs. They tugged and tugged on the free end of the knotted rope until Tuley was finally able to step onto dry land.

Tuley shook off the mud and sand, splattering the entire crew in the process.

"Hey!" Kherrington whined.

Tired, they all rested a minute and drank water. But they realized that the sun was beginning to set as they heard the buzzing of razor insects in the distance.

Chapter 10

"The Destination"

"Tuley! It's getting dark! We have to go!" Bingo said frantically. As Tuley stood, he could see the razor insects coming in their direction.

"I'm not afraid of those little razor insects or The Sashquashawon," Tuley trumpeted.

Gizmo was inspired by Tuley's bravery. "If you're not afraid, then I'm not afraid," he declared. "I'll stand and fight with you!"

"That's what I'm talking about! I'm tired of running!" Captain Toussaint yelled. "Let's stand and fight!"

They were ready to stand together and fight the razor insects and The Sashquashawon. That made Bingo remember a time, long ago, when he scared the razor insects away with fire. He told the group and they quickly moved to gather dry sticks and bushes to make fire sticks.

Tuley moved toward the quicksand pit and filled his trunk with mud. When the insects got close enough, he sprayed the mud into the swarm of bugs. The mud stuck to their wings as many of them started to fall out of the sky.

Bingo and the crew chased the remaining insects with their fire sticks. The razor insects retreated and scattered away.

The Sashquashawon charged from behind the razor insects. He was up next. He stood eight-feet tall with orangish-brown fur that was layered overtop of his purple skin and had six, piercing green eyes, fangs and claws. The Sashquashawon would certainly strike fear into even the bravest beings.

Everyone looked scared except Tuley. Tuley looked over at Bingo and said, "Don't worry, I got this." He then charged straight at The Sashquashawon. He crashed into the scary beast with a boom that resounded throughout the entire island. The Sashquashawon flipped into the air, fell to the ground, and then got back up to rush toward Tuley again.

The two creatures began to battle furiously.

"Go ahead without me," Tuley ordered. "You need to make it to the fountains before dark."

"But Tuley, you wanted to go the fountains, too!" Kherrington protested.

Tuley knew that he no longer needed to go to the fountains. He just wanted to make some friends. And he had found them with their crew and wanted them to be safe above all else.

"I'll be okay," he told them, urging his friends to go on as he crashed his tusks into The Sashquashawon.

Captain Toussaint told the crew to follow him as he ran toward the sound of the fountains. As they ran the sun began to set.

When the sun was almost down, Bingo saw the fountains and pointed toward them. The fountains glimmered and shined with a colorful glow. The sight was so amazing that Captain Toussaint stopped in his tracks. All he could do was admire the view of the most beautiful cascading water he had ever seen.

"Let's go Captain, we don't have much time," Bingo said, nudging and shaking the captain until he snapped out of his daze.

The sun was nearly down and they were only a few feet away from the water. They ran as fast as they could and dove in.

Once they had made it, they splashed and played in the water and drank some of it, too. It was the best feeling ever until they started to feel tired again.

"I'm starting to feel the same way I felt in the flowers," Kherrington commented. Then she yawned just before passing out. She hit the ground with a thud, right where the fountain water had dried up. The rest of the crew did the same and they all passed out instantly.

Bingo and Gizmo were the only two who remained awake. They gave each other a fearful and puzzled look. They both wondered what just happened. They had never seen anyone pass out after bathing in the fountains.

Gizmo and Bingo tried feverishly to wake the crew, but to no avail, they remained deep asleep.

"This was supposed to help them find their purpose," Bingo whimpered.

Gizmo hung his head low and didn't know what to do. They both felt sad. But then in the background, they heard Tuley blowing his trunk in their direction victoriously. He had beaten The Sashquashawon. That lifted Bingo and Gizmo's spirits.

"Boy are we happy to see you," Gizmo told him.

"I told you that I'd take care of him! I'm a little banged up but I'll be alright," Tuley said. He then saw the sleeping crew. "What happened to them? Did they make it to the fountains in time?"

"Yes, we made it here just in the nick of time. But they all fell asleep after bathing in the water, and we can't seem to wake them," Bingo explained.

"Put them on my back," Tuley said. "We better find shelter. We know Dr. Z and his minions are probably lurking somewhere nearby. I know a good hiding place not far from here."

It took a little while before Tuley had finally carried the sleeping crew to the bottom of the cliffs. But when they didn't find any shelter, Gizmo grew nervous.

"Is this it? Are we supposed to just sit here and wait for Dr. Z's army to come get us?" he said angrily.

Tuley placed the crew gently on the ground. "There is a cave just behind this boulder," he said with exhaustion.

He started to push on a huge boulder at the base of the cliff. It took all of his strength to move the boulder from in front of the cave entrance. They entered the cave and took the crew inside. Bingo even found some leftover dried fruit and nuts that had been stashed in the cave.

Once they were safe, Tuley, Gizmo, and Bingo fell asleep, waiting and hoping to see what would happen tomorrow.

Chapter 11

"Now What"

The night was quiet. There was no more buzzing from the razor insects or roaring and scratching from The Sashquashawon. Everyone slept soundly except Bingo. He tossed and turned and thought about how and why the crew had fallen into this deep sleep. The concern weighed heavy on his mind. He had never seen anything like that before. Eventually, he fell asleep.

As the morning approached, everyone started to feel the heat from the sun. A small speck of light shimmered through the cave. Bingo awoke immediately and ran over to the crew to check on them.

He started to hoot in his monkey language and lifted Kherrington's arm. But it only fell back to the floor with a thud. She was obviously still in a deep sleep.

He then checked on Captain Toussaint by poking him with a stick and shouting, "Captain, wake up now!"

The Captain didn't move. Bingo had no luck waking their mother or father either. He then walked over and sat on a stone. He hung his head and started to cry.

Tuley and Gizmo heard his sobs and asked him what was

wrong.

"It's all my fault," Bingo answered between sobs. "I told them that if they went to the fountains, they'd find their purpose and be able to return to their ship. But look at them now."

Gizmo tried to reassure his friend. "They're still alive, just sleeping. Maybe they'll find their purpose in their dreams."

"Yeah, just calm down," Tuley agreed. "I have a feeling that everything is going to be okay. Now that the sun is up, maybe we can take them back to the fountains."

Bingo jumped up excitedly. "That's a great idea! Maybe we'll take them and put them back into the water."

Still recovering from his battle with The Sashquashawon, Tuley didn't think he'd be able to carry the sleeping crew again. So Bingo and Gizmo gathered two long, strong sticks, some rope, and a blanket. They used the rope to tie the blanket to both sticks and made a pallet. Then they moved the sleeping crew onto the blanket of the newly built contraption.

Gizmo and Bingo each picked up sticks and began to drag them, while Tuley followed behind them.

After pulling the four crew members a considerable distance, Gizmo and Bingo began to tire. They struggled with every step. Nevertheless, they were determined to get the crew back to the fountains. Eventually, they approached the bend just before the water. Filled with anticipation, they turned the corner and were devastated to find that the fountains were no longer there.

Gizmo, Bingo, and Tuley all plopped down in defeat as Bingo started to cry again. As he sobbed, they began to hear the whirl of a machine. It made a loud long buzzing noise, sounding like an electronic bumblebee. And it was moving toward them.

As the machine got closer, Bingo, Tuley and Gizmo spotted their longtime nemesis, Dr. Z, in a hovercraft. He was a pale, balding man who relied on a respirator to breathe. Normally, the trio would have run away or hid from him. But they were so disheartened that they didn't bother to move.

Dr. Z pulled his hovercraft close to them and smiled an evil smile. Then he bellowed with a menacing laugh, "Heh, heh, heh, heh, heh. Well, well, well. If it isn't Bingo, Gizmo and Tuley. What an odd group of characters. And who are these sleeping beauties you have here with you?"

"I'm sure you already know who they are," Bingo answered angrily.

Dr. Z laughed even harder. "You're so right! You thought these people would be able to save you, but now you'll remain under my rule."

Tuley let out a thunderous, trumpeting roar from his trunk. It was so loud that it rattled Dr. Z's machine and made it malfunction.

"You're going to pay for that!" Dr. Z shouted angrily. "I'll have my minions to deal with you all shortly."

"Go ahead and get your minions. I don't care anymore," Bingo responded. He threw stones from the ground as Dr. Z's machine struggled to stay afloat. Gizmo and Tuley joined in with the rock throwing.

Dr. Z banged on his hovercraft to get it to move away.

"I'll be back!" he yelled as he sped off.

"He can go get all the minions he wants. I'm tired of running," Bingo said defiantly. Gizmo and Tuley became angry as well.

"I'm gonna call all of my friends to come here to help us defeat Dr. Z once and for all," Tuley decided.

"Wait, a minute," Gizmo said. "I thought you didn't have any friends."

"Well, maybe not friends, but I do know lots of other creatures who are all tired of Dr. Z and his goons. Maybe they'll all come out and join us!"

"Yeah, well, call them then," Bingo told him. "We'll gather everyone on the island to join in."

Gizmo and Bingo built a big fire so the smoke would draw a crowd of the other jungle animals. Tuley went to the top of the mountain and bellowed as loud as he could with his trunk.

Within an hour, all the island creatures had gathered with them where the fountains used to be. There were small animals that looked like squirrels, several graffiti skinned rhinoceros, birds, and insects that could walk and talk.

The jungle was filled with a whole host of unusual island inhabitants.

Bingo climbed aboard Tuley's back to give them all a speech.

"Dear friends, I don't know about you but I'm sick of Dr. Z and his minions controlling my life and making me live in fear!"

The crowd of animals and plants roared in agreement.

Bingo pointed to the sleeping crew of humans and explained the story of their journey. He told them about their deep sleep and how he suspected that Dr. Z was somehow responsible for it.

The crowd gasped with fear and admiration as Bingo told the story of how they had chased Dr. Z away earlier by throwing rocks at his hovercraft.

"Don't be afraid! If we stick together we can defeat Dr. Z and his goons," he told them all. "Just like we did with The Sashquashawon!"

A collective gasp came over the crowd.

An animal from the back of the crowd came forward. "The Sashquashawon?"

"Yes, The Sashquashawon," Tuley declared proudly. "I destroyed him all by myself!"

The crowd broke out into applause before Bingo told them of his plan to defeat Dr. Z. "So gather your rocks and sticks to fight him," he commanded. "And when Dr. Z returns, we'll be ready for him."

Chapter 12

"Courage"

Everyone roared with excitement and began to chant, "Bring Dr. Z! Bring Dr. Z! Bring Dr. Z!"

They began stomping and banging their weapons of sticks and rocks on the ground. They stomped so hard that the ground began to shake. No one noticed that Captain Toussaint and the crew were starting to stir from their sleep.

Suddenly, the sky filled with a big, black cloud that headed straight toward them. It was Dr. Z and his evil friends. They were approaching on the ground and in the air; razor insects, robots and reptiles. And they were running and riding hovercrafts directly toward Bingo and the other animals.

Some of the animals began to back off, feeling nervous and scared. Bingo could see it in their faces, so he jumped on top of Tuley's back again to encourage the crowd.

"If you are tired of being scared, if you are tired of Dr. Z's nonsense, then this is not the time to be afraid. It is the time to fight!" he proclaimed. The animals and plants then roared with excitement as Dr. Z's army of bad guys barreled down on them.

Tuley began battling and beating the robots, insects and reptiles left and right. The other animals began to feel like they could defeat Dr. Z as they battled his minions.

But when a second wave of Dr. Z's army bumrushed the crowd, the jungle plants and animals stopped fighting. They no longer felt they could win. Dr. Z could sense the fear in them.

"You silly animals! Don't you know I control you? I'm gonna make you *pay* for standing up for yourselves!" he mocked them. "My machines will destroy and crush all of your hope."

As his second wave of goons approached, many of the plants and animals began to run away. Gizmo, Tuley and Bingo tried to stop them.

"Don't run, don't run! Stay and fight!" they shouted. But the other animals continued to run.

Dr. Z's beasts and machines overpowered Bingo, Gizmo and Tuley and the three were captured.

"Now I'm going to make a public display of you three," Dr. Z promised.

He sent out an announcement over a bullhorn. "To all of you animals that stood up to me, I'm gonna give you one last chance to redeem yourselves! Come here tomorrow at high noon and pledge your allegiance to me, and all will be forgiven!"

He sped off to his lair with his three prisoners as he conjured up different ways to punish them.

While the animals and plants battled Dr. Z and his army, Captain Toussaint and his crew began to awake. But with the animals in hiding and Tuley, Bingo, and Gizmo captured, they fell back in a deep sleep.

At Dr. Z's lair, Tuley, Gizmo and Bingo sulked at being captured and locked in a dark dungeon, but then they began to joke with one another to cheer themselves up.

"Wow, I can't believe it will all end tomorrow. But we stood up to that evil Dr. Z," Bingo said proudly.

The three of them thought about how they had stood up to Dr. Z and they grew encouraged. Their confidence attracted a lightning bug to the tiny window that allowed air into the room. The more excitement they felt about standing up to Dr. Z, the brighter the lightning bug shined. And as they joked and laughed, the firefly's light began to change colors. Bingo even complimented the twinkling bug.

"Your lights are very beautiful," he said. "Thank you for spending this time with us and shining some light on what could've been a very dark day. Go and shine your light throughout the jungle and tell the others we're not angry with them for running away."

On its mission, the lightning bug flew away to shine its light around the entire jungle. All of the animals, plants and trees were amazed at the beauty of the firefly. Its colors were constantly changing and shining brightly.

The animals and plants felt a sense of hope, despite Dr. Z's promise to return and make them all submit to his will.

Eventually, the lightning bug made it to the sleeping crew of humans who remained alongside the vanished fountains and began to dance around them with its colorful glow.

Chapter 13

"Hope and Victory"

*T*he lightning bug continued to dance rhythmically around the crew as if it was trying to wake them. With its array of changing colors, it gave the most amazing light show ever. The crew remained asleep, but their bodies swayed along with the rhythm of the firefly. The bug then landed on Captain Toussaint's nose.

When the firefly landed on the captain's nose, it magically woke him up, and made him aware of everything that happened while they were asleep, like a transfer of information.

"Yes! It's time. This isn't over," the captain said excitedly. He knew exactly what they needed to do. "We're going to free our friends and defeat Dr. Z. And I thank you for helping us," he said with gratitude to the lightning bug.

The bug danced around the other crew members, and one by one, they all started to awake.

After waking up the crew, the bug continued on his mission, displaying its miraculous light show. The lightning bug had brought a new spirit of hope to the jungle.

Finally wide awake, the crew began to roam the entire island, preparing all of the animals and plants for a battle to free their friends.

"Be encouraged, we are awake now and will free our friends tomorrow," Captain Toussaint shouted. "Stand with us and do not be afraid!"

The animals and plants were all in disbelief that the human crew members were suddenly awake.

"They're the ones who were sent here to free us, but weren't they in a deep sleep?" one of the graffiti-skinned rhinoceros asked.

"I thought they'd never wake up," a squirrel said in surprise.

The crew asked them all to join them in defeating Dr. Z once and for all. "Dr. Z said to meet him here in this desert tomorrow at high noon. Well, we're going to do just that," Captain Toussaint told them.

He advised the animals to gather objects from the forest and build imitations of themselves to fool Dr. Z. So when Dr. Z arrived, he would believe that they were all in the crowd instead of hiding. The captain also instructed the animals to dig small holes with ladders where they could hide underground. They also dug huge, deep holes to trap Dr. Z's machines.

All of the animals worked hard throughout the night to prepare. And as daytime began to break, Captain Toussaint instructed the animals to rest up.

"We are now ready for the fight to free our friends and get rid of Dr. Z!" he howled with excitement.

Later that morning, and just before noon, Dr. Z and his crew headed toward the meeting place where the animals had gathered. As his clan got closer, the crowd of animals and plants roared and shouted repeatedly, "End them! End them! End Bingo, Gizmo and Tuley!"

They wanted to make Dr. Z think that they were all on his side. And their shouts gave Dr. Z more confidence.

"I have the traitors here with me!" Dr. Z proclaimed over a loudspeaker. He then rolled out a cage near the holes the animals had dug. Inside the cage were Bingo, Gizmo and Tuley. But their faces no longer showed fear or dispair.

"Here they are. You see them? You'll now see what becomes of those who oppose me," Dr. Z shouted. "I'm going to release my razor insects to slice them up before turning them into dust with my new invention."

Just as Dr. Z was about to release the razor insects into the cage, Captain Toussaint blew a horn. Immediately, a group of animals rushed toward Dr. Z and caught him and his clan off guard.

Totally surprised by it, and outnumbered, Dr. Z and his army started running away. "Retreat, retreat!" he screamed.

Instead of getting away, Dr. Z's minions and robots fell into the pits that the animals had dug for them. The animals and plants then hurled rocks and sticks nonstop at the rest of Dr. Z's army. Another group of animals started a ring of fire to trap the razor insects inside.

But Dr. Z remained determined to destroy Tuley, Bingo, and Gizmo. He reached for the start button on his invention and pressed it. The machine began to close in on the trio as the crew smashed rocks on the glass of the apparatus. Unfortunately, they were unsuccessful. The crew then tried to burn the machine while hitting it with more useless stones.

Sadly, it looked as if their island friends were about to be destroyed.

But then a big, beautiful and powerful bird swooped down and snatched the machine controls from Dr. Z's hand and dropped it into the hands of First Mate Kherrington.

Not knowing how to work it, she began to randomly push buttons, making the machine move even faster. Finally, she hit the right button that shut the machine down.

Realizing that they were winning the battle, their mother began to sing another powerful and triumphant song. The plants, flowers and trees grew once more, responding to her voice like they did before in the desert.

There was one tree in particular that grew close to the glass cage that held Bingo, Gizmo, and Tuley. As the tree began to grow, its branches and limbs broke through the glass and freed their friends. The more she sang, the more the trees grew.

Soon, the tree vines began to attack Dr. Z's machines, while tying up the rest of his army. The trees even grabbed Dr. Z's hovercraft and took it high into the sky toward the clouds before dropping it back to the ground.

Dr. Z's machine then swooshed to the bottom of one of the deep pits where it crashed and exploded.

Knowing that they had lost the battle, Dr. Z's remaining crew took off and ran away.

The animals roared, cheered, and cried with excitement and joy after a hard-fought victory!

Chapter 14

"Going Home"

The animals and plants continued to celebrate. They danced, jumped, yelled and swayed with joy. As they danced, Bingo and Captain Toussaint looked toward the sky and saw a cloud filled with a shimmering light. They caught each other's eyes, thinking and wondering to themselves what it meant.

Captain Toussaint asked everyone to be quiet so he could have a moment to speak. "Well, I guess we found our purpose," he said to Bingo.

The crowd was puzzled. "So what was it?" the crowd asked.

"To encourage you all to stand up to Dr. Z and regain control of your lives and fate!"

The crowd broke out in cheers and jubilation with Bingo.

He said, "I told ya," and let out anther monkey howl. *"Oooh, oooh, oooh, oooh, oooh, oooh, euuuww!"*

Kherrington exclaimed, "Tomorrow, when we wake up, we can return to our ship."

Gizmo and Tuley became sad at the thought of their new friends leaving, so did Bingo. Feeling their sadness, their mom said, "But tonight, let's celebrate and not worry about tomorrow until tomorrow comes."

The group smiled and focused on their celebration for the rest of the day. In the late-night hours, the party finally wound down and everyone fell asleep.

When the sun rose the next morning, the crew said their goodbyes to Bingo, Gizmo, and Tuley.

"We made great friends here during this journey, but we must return home," Captain Toussaint told them sadly.

Although their new animal friends understood, they remained saddened to see them go.

"Well, come on we'll show you the way," Bingo finally said.

They began to make their trek back through the jungle until they reached a clearing of a cliff. From the cliff, they could see their ship in the water. The crew was overjoyed to find it again.

"Now we just have to figure out how to get down there," their dad stated.

"That's easy," Tuley told them, pointing with his trunk. "Just take this path down the cliff. You'll reach the beach, and from there you'll be able to make it back to your ship with ease."

The crew headed quickly toward the path as Bingo and Gizmo joined them, but Tuley was too big to go. They made their way down the winding path of the cliff to the beach and finally touched the sand. With each step on the sand, a sad, yet triumphant song played until they had finally reached the edge of the sea.

Bingo pointed to the small boat that would take the crew back to their ship. He and Gizmo then gave each of the crew members a big hug.

Holding back tears, Bingo gave Captain Toussaint a map. "This should guide you back to your home." Then he pulled out a compass and handed it to the Captain as well.

"Any time you see the purple star in the sky shimmering, you'll know that we are thinking of you and know that we're looking forward to seeing you again," Bingo said.

"Purple star? Kherrington responded in confusion. "There aren't any purple stars."

"Yeah, and there aren't any talking bears and monkeys

either," Gizmo responded with a smile.

The whole group laughed.

"The last thing you must remember is that you drank the magical waters," Bingo told them. "That means you'll be able to see things that others cannot, even when you return home."

With that, the crew hopped into the small boat and rowed it toward their pirate ship. They climbed aboard, loaded up their supplies, and raised the anchor to sail away. Then they looked back and waved goodbye to their island friends; Bingo, Gizmo, and Tuley, who continued to watch them from up high on the cliff.

When their ship was far enough in the distance, where they could no longer see the human crew, Bingo, Gizmo, and Tuley turned toward the jungle and headed back to their homes with confidence that someday, somehow, they would all see their friends again.

The End

Meet Dr. Darius M. Walker

Dr. Darius M. Walker is a dedicated husband and loving father of two wonderful children under the age of 10. Professionally trained in scientific writing through his Doctoral studies in Biophysics and Genetics, Darius displays the ability to draft difficult concepts. Dr. Walker has enhanced his writing skills through his research administration and technology innovation career track. He combines his technical writing expertise with his artistic side, demonstrated through originally composed poetry and hip-hop lyrics displayed at various open-mic venues as a young adult. Drawing on the art of freestyling and storytelling, along with his love for family –Dr. Walker develops stories to excite the minds of children. Ornamenting colorful vocabulary with nuanced technical and historical information, Darius enables children to have fun while expanding their capacity to learn.

Growing up in the small city of Harrisburg, PA followed by stints in Atlanta, GA, Denver, CO, Gaithersburg, MD and now the Middle East (Doha, Qatar) has given Dr. Walker the unique ability to speak universally to people of varying backgrounds through his writing. His time as a substitute teacher and counselor for at-risk youth also contributes to his ability to connect with children and adolescents on an array of subject matters. As a proud member of Omega Psi Phi, Fraternity Inc., Dr. Walker incorporates the principles and culture of perseverance and uplift within his writing to help shape determination and teamwork among young minds.

Library of Qatar Number: 531/2020
ISBN: 9789927401213